Davis & Lawrence

Nursing the sick : practical information by a trained nurse ;

directions for amateur nursing at home

Davis & Lawrence

Nursing the sick : practical information by a trained nurse ; directions for amateur nursing at home

ISBN/EAN: 9783742844613

Manufactured in Europe, USA, Canada, Australia, Japa

Cover: Foto ©Andreas Hilbeck / pixelio.de

Manufactured and distributed by brebook publishing software
(www.brebook.com)

Davis & Lawrence

Nursing the sick : practical information by a trained nurse ;

directions for amateur nursing at home

NURSING THE SICK

BY A TRAINED NURSE

DIRECTIONS

FOR

AMATEUR

NURSING

AT HOME

SIXTH
EDITION

PUBLISHED BY

DAVIS & LAWRENCE CO., LTD.

MONTREAL AND NEW YORK.

The D. & L.
Menthol Plaster

FOR THE EFFECTUAL and PERMANENT RELIEF OF PAIN

Most Wonderful PLASTER

in the World.

CURES

NERVE DISORDERS, PAIN and STITCHES,
RHEUMATISM, NEURALGIA, PLEURISY,
HEADACHE, PAIN IN THE SIDE,
and is the ANTI-RHEUMATIC
PLASTER OF THE AGE.

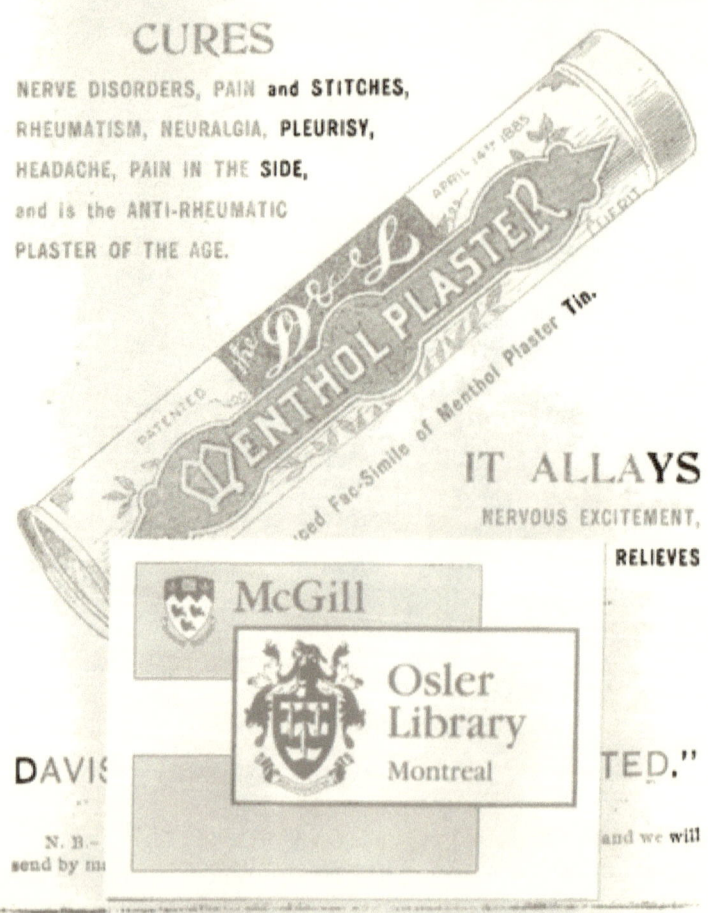

IT ALLAYS

NERVOUS EXCITEMENT,

RELIEVES

DAVIS ... TED."

N. B.— ... and we will
send by ma...

NURSING THE SICK

PRACTICAL INFORMATION

BY A

TRAINED NURSE

DIRECTIONS FOR AMATEUR NURSING AT HOME.

ENTERED according to Act of the Parliament of Canada, in the year 1897 by
DAVIS & LAWRENCE CO., LTD., at the Department of Agriculture.

PUBLISHED BY

DAVIS & LAWRENCE CO., Ltd.

MONTREAL

1897.

PREFACE.

This little book is issued by the publishers with the hope that it will prove an acceptable acquisition to every household in which it may find its way. It is full of valuable information and is written in a plain, concise and accurate manner by one in the profession and we are sure that it will be felt as a " friend in need " in all cases of sickness or disease with which it treats. It deals with all the principles to be observed in nursing the sick and gives accurate instructions of how to carry them out. There is a chapter on " Nursing at Home," which deals in generalties only, a chapter on " Ventilation," which gives very explicit directions how to supply the sick room with pure fresh air without exposing the patient to draughts, and thereby endangering his life, and other equally important instructions on this subject. Then there are chapters on how to " bathe " a sick person, the care of the " bed," how to prepare all kinds of " poultices," " stimulating applications," on " Food " and how to prepare it, as well as chapters upon "Accidents," " Emergencies " and " Disinfection," each and every subject being carefully and fully explained. Making it very simple and easy to carry out by the most inexperienced person, and we feel confident that it will be highly appreciated by all those who need such instructions in the care of the sick.

DAVIS & LAWRENCE CO., Ltd.

Montreal, January 1898.

NURSING AT HOME.

CHAPTER I.

NURSING AT HOME.

IN the care of the sick, the nurse is second in importance only to the doctor. Very often as far as the comfort of the patient is concerned, she occupies the first place. The doctor comes, prescribes, and goes. It is many hours before the patient sees him again, and in the meanwhile he is left to the tender mercies of the nurse.

However wise and judicious the doctor's method of treatment may be, the full effect cannot be obtained unless it is intelligently carried out. If he orders a poultice, in inflammation of the lungs, he wants a warm, soft mass of the proper consistency applied, so that it shall not soil the skin or clothing of the patient. He wants it changed at regular intervals, and in such a way as not to give the sufferer cold every time it is removed. Unless the nurse knows how to manage it, the poultice is likely to do as much harm as good.

Let any woman ask herself, "could I give a bath to a person in bed without wetting the clothing or change the under sheet while the bed was occupied?" and she will smile at the seeming impossibility. When once she is shown how to do it, she only wonders that she did not discover the right way herself. Sick persons in well-to-do families are sometimes allowed to wear the same clothing for a week and to remain unwashed during a long illness, because the friends believe it impossible to care for them without injuring them.

In this little book, practical directions are given for the performance of all these necessary offices. The knowledge of any of them is not taken for granted, and the writer has tried to do it in such a plain and simple manner that no one need mistake the easiest way.

CHAPTER II.

VENTILATION.

THE first requisite in the sick room is pure air. Emanations from the body and the breath of the patient are constantly tainting it, and it must be removed or else the soiled air is inhaled over and over again, poisoning both **sufferer and** nurse. Fresh air can be admitted only through the windows. Two points must be observed. Supply heat to keep the room at a proper temperature, and protect the sick person from draughts. Those in bed rarely take cold—never, if properly protected.

Lower the window at the top a few inches. If the upper sash is not made to open, remove the cleats underneath it and move them down the required distance.

Where the upper and lower sash lap, there is a space which admits a constant current of fresh air. If the bed is near the window, place a screen between them. If the weather is too cold to permit of the window being kept open, cover the patient's head and all, with an extra blanket, and open the window three or four times a day, keeping on the extra covering until the room is warm again.

If a room is cold, it is no sign the air is fresh. Cold air may have been breathed over and over until it is as impure as warm air. The only safety lies in constantly changing the air. A thermometer should hang in every sick room and the temperature be kept at 68°, except in fever, and then at 65°. An open fire is the best heat producer, because it helps to carry the bad air up the chimney and acts as a ventilator as well. In summer, place a lighted lamp in the fire place, or if there is a stove-pipe hole in the chimney, take the tin stopper out of it. When the room is heated by a stove, a coil of pipes, or a register, keep a saucepan of boiling water on it to give off steam to moisten the air.

In order to keep the air pure, no vessel that has been used must be allowed to remain in the room, a moment longer than is absolutely necessary. A little disinfectant solution should be kept standing in them. Covers should be provided, and the moment the patient has finished using one, it should be carried away and emptied, well scalded with boiling water and rinsed in the disinfectants. Vessels of the proper shape for use in bed can be obtained at a small expense, and no sick person should be allowed to get out of bed for any purpose whatever. It exhausts the strength unnecessarily and is a fruitful source of colds. The India rubber bed pans and urinals are very valuable, particularly the former, **for** use when the sufferer is thin and cannot bear the contact with **the hard** surface of an earthen one. They require to be rinsed in a strong solution of chloride of lime or carbolic acid after each using.

If possible, the carpets should be removed from the floor and the surface wiped every day with a damp cloth wrung out of a solution of corrosive sublimate. The woodwork should be dusted with a similar cloth, and any article of furniture lightly gone over with the same. This makes the room perfectly fresh and sweet. If the carpet cannot be taken up, sweep with a carpet sweeper or a broom covered with a cloth dampened in corrosive sublimate, and burn the dust. Remove curtains from windows and bed, all draperies and unnecessary pieces of furniture, to leave no hiding place for dust. Perfect cleanliness does much towards keeping the air in the room pure.

CHAPTER III.

BATHING.

NLESS the doctor specially forbids it, a sick person should have a bath every day. This keeps open the pores of the skin, and enables the system to throw off through them a vast amount of waste matter which cannot be retained in the body without injury to it. A sponge bath can be easily and quickly given without causing an undue amount of fatigue.

Before beginning, collect at the bedside all the things that will be needed : two blankets, two towels, a basin of tepid water, a pitcher of warm water to replenish it as it cools, a wash cloth and soap, *Palmo-Tar* or *Palmo Sulphur soaps* are valuable in diseases **of** the skin, and *Palmo-Carbolic* soap in any infectious diseases, as **scarlet fever** or measles. They can be obtained at any drug store. If the **night** clothes are to be changed, have the clean ones, aired and warmed, **close** at hand.

Fold one of the blankets end to end, and beginning at the ends roll it about half its width. Move the patient over to one side of the bed and tuck the upper bed clothes around him. On the cleared space lay the blanket with the roll toward the patient. Tuck the free edge under the mattress. Lift the patient over the roll on the blanket. Unroll it on the other side. Lay the second blanket over the upper bed clothes, and, holding it in place with one hand, draw them away underneath it, leaving the patient covered with it alone. A second blanket can be added if one seems to light a covering.

To remove the night-dress draw it up at the back until the whole length lies in folds under the neck. Lay the arms above the head, on the pillow. Raise the head with one hand, and with the other, slip the folds over the head, holding them gathered in the hand for the purpose. Keep the upper blanket well up to the chin, and under its shelter draw the night-dress off the arms and take it away. Bathe the face, neck and ears carefully, and dry them. Pass the hand holding the wash-cloth under the blanket and wash one arm ; wipe it, and then do the other. When this is finished bathe the chest, turn the patient on the side and do the back ; also the back of the thighs, drying each part before wetting the next. Turn again on the back and bathe the front of the thighs, the **legs and** feet. Attend carefully to the nails, paring them if necessary.

When it is desired to change the under sheet, have the clean one rolled half **way** across from side to side. Lay the roll next the patient, pushing the soiled sheet before it. Tuck the free edge under the mattress, lay the patient on the smooth place, go to the other side of the bed, pull off soiled sheet, unroll the fresh one, and tuck the edge in firmly.

To change the upper sheet without exposing the patient, lay the clean one on top of the bed clothes with a blanket over it, and draw them out underneath it.

Wash the teeth with a clean rag dipped in borax water, or what is still better, get from your druggist a bottle of Alkaline and Antiseptic Tablets. They are cleansing and very refreshing.

When the lips or skin are rough or chapped, moisten them with Hind's Honey and Almond Cream, and repeat the application several times in the day.

In bathing a baby that is afraid of water, place a small blanket over the tub, lay the child on it and gently lower it into the water.

When sponge baths are given to reduce the heat of the body in fever, Alcohol or Bay rum is added to the water, and the skin is not dried because the moisture evaporating helps to cool it.

CHAPTER IV.

THE BED.

THE best bed for a sick person is a wire woven mattress with a soft hair mattress over it. A feather bed should not be used if it is possible to avoid it.

To make the bed, spread a clean sheet on the mattress, tuck it under and pin it at the four corners underneath the mattress. This keeps it smooth and tight, an important point **in the** prevention of bed sores.

Rubber sheeting can be **bought by the yard, and** is not expensive. Have a strip one yard wide **and long** enough to lie across the bed, and tuck well under on each side. Fold this strip in a sheet, and place it in the middle of the bed, pinning the ends under the mattress on each side. This saves the lower sheet, and can be easily changed with very little disturbance to the patient.

Tuck the top sheet in at the foot of the bed and leave the sides **free.** Add as many blankets as are required, but no more. Florence Nightingale says, "Feverishness is supposed to be a symptom of fever; nine times out of ten it is a symptom of bedding."

Have one or two pillows as required. Do **not** let the invalid lie with his head in a hole. Turn the pillows **frequently** to present a cool, fresh surface to the hot face.

If the sufferer is very thin, a long, narrow pillow placed between the legs to prevent the knees from touching, prevents chafing. When the bed is frequently wet or soiled, it is well to keep an old sheet folded several times under the patient or, to use a small one as a napkin, arranging it like a child's. In these cases, special attention must be paid to washing, drying and powdering the parts touched by the discharges.

BED SORES
Continued pressure on any part of the body stops the circulation of the blood through it, and as no nourishment is carried to it, the tissue dies. This is the reason why bed sores form in those places where the weight rests as the sick person lies in bed. The lower part of the spine, the hips, elbows and heels must be bathed every day with alcohol, and when that dries off, powdered with cornstarch. This helps to toughen the skin. The moment any redness appears, a wash made of equal parts of Goulard Water and Tincture of Catechu, which can be obtained from any druggist, should be used to still further harden it.

The patient must be frequently turned on one side, to give the affected parts relief. If he is too weak for this, then a rubber cushion, with a hole in the middle, must be placed under him, so that the sore spot will rest over the hole. Thick pillows can be arranged above and below, to take the weight off it, if a rubber cushion cannot **be** had.

Keeping the cross sheet free from crumbs, the patient **dry, well** rubbed with alcohol and powdered, and when possible, **frequent** change of position, will usually prevent them.

If, in spite of every precaution, the skin shows signs **of cracking,** rub it with oxide of zinc ointment, and relieve it from **pressure at** any cost.

If matter forms, wash it every day with water containing a little carbolic acid, and dress it with the oxide of zinc or boro glyceride ointment, spread on a piece of soft linen fastened on with strips of adhesive plaster. Do not let this plaster cross the sore, but strap it along the sides of the square of the linen, leaving it long enough to take a firm hole on the well skin beyond.

Bed sores often take away the patient's last chance of life, by exhausting his strength, so precautions against them cannot be taken too soon. The points to be remembered are, keep the under sheet smooth and dry ; change the position several times a day ; **if** this cannot be done, arrange something to take the pressure off the **part.**

CHAPTER V.

POULTICES.

FLAXSEED meal is the best material for poultices. Have a sufficient quantity of water boiling in a saucepan ; a pint is enough to make a good sized poultice. Stir in handfuls of the meal until the mass is thick enough not to run when spread, but not too stiff. It need not boil. Have ready a square of cotton about two inches larger each way than the poultice is to be when finished. Spread the flaxseed on this about half an inch thick, leaving a margin of cotton all around it. Turn this margin up on the poultice like a hem to prevent its running out. Have a square of cheese cloth or muslin to lay over the poultice, to prevent the flaxseed from touching the skin.

If it is not applied to a discharging wound the flaxseed can be scraped off the cotton into the sauce-pan when it is cold, and heated again, more water being added if it is too stiff, or meal if it is too thin.

When onions are ordered, bake them until tender, mash with a spoon, spred on the cotton, cover with muslin, and apply.

MEN'S SURGICAL WARD—IN A MODERN HOSPITAL.

A poultice should always be changed before it gets cold, once in two hours is a good rule if they are not ordered oftener. Have the fresh one ready to put on before removing the other, and bring it to the bedside rolled up on a hot plate to keep it warm.

When a poultice is discontinued, dry the skin thoroughly, and cover the part with one or two thicknesses of flannel.

A poultice jacket is made of oiled muslin lined with cotton batting. Have it in two pieces to cover the back and chest, and fasten on the shoulders and under the arms with strings. Put the poultices on underneath it, making them as large as is necessary.

It is a good plan to cover any poultice with a newspaper, folded in flannel, to keep in the heat. If weight is no objection an India Rubber Hot Water Bag, half filled with hot water, can be laid over it. This prevents the need of changing it so frequently.

FOMEN-TATIONS. These are lighter than poultices, and more quickly got ready. They must be changed very often as they cool almost immediately. Provide two pieces of flannel large enough to be folded once, a stout towel, a basin, and a kettle of boiling water. Lay the towel in the basin with the ends hanging over the sides, in the middle of it place one piece of the flannel folded, pour on enough boiling water to cover it. Take the dry ends of the towel, one in each hand, and twist them in opposite directions at the same time lifting it out of the water. This will squeeze it perfectly dry, without burning the hands. Untwist the towel, take out the hot, moist flannel, shake it and lay it on the patient. After the fomentations are discontinued, dry the part and cover it with warm, dry flannel. See that the night-dress and sheet are not wet.

Sometimes mustard is added to the water when there is great pain ; a heaping teaspoonful to the pint. The mustard water can be heated more than once.

DRY HEAT. A hot water bottle is invaluable as a means of applying dry heat. Persons who suffer from sleeplessness usually have cold feet. The hot water bottle relieves this symptom by drawing the blood to them. The pressure on the brain being lessened, sleep follows. The steady heat is very soothing to sufferers from rheumatism, neuralgia, face-ache, or ear-ache. The plain ones should be wrapped in a towel before applying.

When a hot water bottle cannot be obtained, a stone jug or a common bottle can be used, but it is a clumsy substitute, and the weight is in many cases a great objection.

CHAPTER VI.

STIMULATING APPLICATIONS.

MEDICINAL plasters come prepared ready to put on, and the nurse has only to follow the directions in applying them. Those of mustard should always be kept in the house for an emergency. If it is a home made one, take **two spoonfuls of mustard** to one of wheat flour, rub them smooth **with a little water, and** with a knife spread the paste **evenly on a square of** cotton. Cover it with a piece of thin muslin, **and turn** the edges up as directed for a poultice. Lay **it on** the part **and** examine it in a few minutes, to see that it is not blistering. As **soon as** the skin is very red, remove it, and wipe the part dry with a soft cloth. Twenty minutes is usually long enough to leave it on. **If the** burning is intense after its removal, dust the place thickly **with flour or toilet powder. The D. & L.** Menthol Plaster is used **with great success in all muscular** pains, stiffness, backache, neuralgia, and rheumatism.

COM-PRESS. Wring a flannel out of hot water, sprinkle **it thickly with Perry** Davis' Pain-Killer and apply. **This is a good appli-**cation, for it does not blister, **and is quickly made** ready.

ENEMAS. To give an enema to a person in bed, lay the patient on the left side, arrange the bed clothes carefully to prevent any unnecessary exposure, place a square of rubber sheeting to catch any drops that may fall. Oil the nozzle and insert it gently. If it meets with any resistance withdraw **it** partially, change the direction a little and try again. For a pur-**gative** enema use from two to four pints of warm soap-suds. Fill **the syringe** once or twice to expel the air before using it, and in-**ject the fluid** very slowly.

After **using,** squeeze clean water through **it a few times, wipe it** and hang it up **by** the open end to dry.

When there is obstinate constipation, salt is added to the water or olive oil mixed with it, four tablespoonfuls to the pint.

Never use oil or turpentine in a soft rubber syringe.

Starch and laudanum are used for prolonged diarrhœa. Thirty **drops** of laudanum to four tablespoonfuls of thin, cold starch.

These are much used in uterine diseases. They can be given with any bulb syringe, a Fountain or combination.

DOUCHES. If one has to be given in bed, as is the case after confinement, raise the hips on pillow or folded **blanket,** place a basin in position if a bed-pan is not obtainable, use the vaginal nozzle. It is dangerous to give a douche with a nozzle perforated at the end, as air **may be** injected into the uterus. The water should flow out as **rapidly as it** flows in, and the douche be continued until it comes away **clear.**

The bed must be protected with a square of rubber **sheeting.**

CHAPTER VII.

LIQUID FOOD.

IN serious illness, the stomach cannot digest solid food, and life has to be supported upon fluids. It is very important that the nurse should know how to prepare a variety, so that the patient may not become disgusted with any one **article** of diet.

Milk alone will sustain life **for a long time.** Sometimes it is too rich and must be diluted with **limewater, or** otherwise prepared for digestion.

To make limewater, **procure a lump of lime, put it in an earthern**
MILK AND jar and **pour coldwater** upon it. **Let it stand until**
LIME- it subsides and the particles of **lime fall to the bot-**
WATER. tom. Pour off the clear liquid, strain **and bottle it.**
The quantity of water put on the lime is of no consequence. **Add two** tablespoonfuls of the lime water to a cup of milk.

This is milk already partially digested by means of its prepara-
PEP- tion with pancreatin. Take about a quarter of a
TONIZED teaspoonful of the pancreatic extract and a pinch of
MILK. common baking soda. Dissolve these in half a cup of water, and add this to one pint of milk. Pour the whole into a bottle and stand it in warm water of a temperature of 110° by the thermometer. Keep the water at this point for half an hour. Remove the bottle and put it on ice to stop the digestive process. If ice cannot be obtained, boil the milk for a minute.

Peptonized milk will be retained when a sensitive stomach would reject it in other forms. Gruel can be peptonized in the same way when it is made with milk.

One quart of fresh milk, a quarter of a compressed yeast cake, **one** tablespoonful of sugar syrup.

KOUMISS. Make the syrup by covering one tablespoonful of sugar with water and boiling a few minutes until clear. Dissolve the yeast cake in warm water. Put this and the syrup into the milk and all into a bottle. Shake well to mix the ingredients thoroughly. Cork with a cork that has previously been soaked in hot water until soft. Drive the cork in well and tie it down with a strong string. Put it in a cool place, a temperature of 52° is desirable, and let it remain for sixty hours. After **that,** keep it in the refrigerator or a dark, cold cellar. Open with a champagne tap, as it flies over everything if the cork is drawn.

It is used with great success in diseases of the stomach, consumption, chronic bronchitis, fevers, and any wasting disease. It helps to produce sleep without leaving any bad after effects.

Albumen is an important part of an invalid's diet, and as white **MILK AND** of egg is nearly pure albumen, it is very valuable. **WHITE OF** It can be given in milk, without the patient being **EGG.** aware of its presence. Put a teacupful of milk and the white of an egg into a bottle, cork tightly and shake for three minutes. A few grains of salt can be added, or sugar if preferred. Water can be substituted for the milk, with a teaspoonful of lemon juice to give it flavor.

Half a pint of milk, one tablespoonful of brandy, or two of whiskey, or three of sherry, a little sugar and grated **MILK** nutmeg. Pour into a bottle, and shake three mi- **PUNCH.** nutes.

Crush two " Rennecine Tablets " and dissolve in a tablespoonful of water, add to one pint of milk slightly warmed, **MILK** a firm curd will be produced. When the curd is set, **WHEY.** break it up with a fork ; let it stand half an hour and **pour** off the whey. Sherry may be added to flavor it if desired, and sugar if it is liked.

Beat an egg light ; stir in a scant teaspoonful of sugar, put it in a glass and fill with milk. A few drops of F yal Ex- **EGG NOG** tract of Vanilla can be added, or the yellow of a lemon rind carefully grated so that none of the white pith comes off with it, this is a pleasant flavoring. It

last, as the alcohol cooks the egg and hardens the sugar if put in before the milk.

Have ready in a saucepan one pint of boiling water. Moisten one heaping tablespoonful of oatmeal with two tablespoonfuls of cold water, add salt, and stir the oatmeal with the boiling water. Let it boil slowly one hour. The gruel can be sweetened or flavored with cinnamon or lemon juice to taste. It can also be made with milk instead of water. If too thick, it can be thinned with milk after it is cooked.

OATMEAL GRUEL.

INDIAN MEAL GRUEL. Make the same as oatmeal gruel without the flavoring. Long, slow boiling is essential to success with gruels.

Wash two tablespoonfuls of rice and boil in one quart of water for an hour. Add lemon juice or Royal Extract of Lemon and sugar to taste, or if sweet is not liked, a little salt or the lemon juice alone.

RICE CREAM.

Neck of beef is the best part for beef tea or beef juice. Cut one pound of meat in inch square pieces removing any particle of fat. Pour over it one pint of cold water and add a little salt. Put it in a saucepan on the back of the stove where it will heat gradually. When it comes to the boiling point, put a hot cover under it and let it stand one hour, hot but not boiling. Pour off the juice, holding back the meat with a spoon. Do not strain it.

BEEF TEA.

Cut half a pound of juicy beef as fine as possible. Cover it with one pint of cold water, add five drops of muriatic acid and a pinch of salt. Let it stand an hour and a half, strain off the juice and give either hot or cold. If heated do not allow it to boil.

BEEF EXTRACT.

Have a thick slice of juicy steak cut from the top of the round. Cut it in strips; hold it on a gridiron over a clear fire for a minute to draw the juice to the surface. Press out the juice with a lemon squeezer or any pressure that can be brought to bear on it.

PURE BEEF JUICE.

Either this recipe or the following one is valuable when nourishment is to be given by enema. Add one grain of pepsin to each tablespoonful of beef juice and let it stand half an hour in warm water at 100° Fahr. This partially digests the food before it enters the bowels, and enables it to be **more** easily absorbed to nourish the body.

OYSTER SOUP. Half a pint of oysters, half a pint of milk, **one** teaspoonful of butter, one dessertspoonful of flour, salt to taste. Melt the butter in a saucepan, add the flour, stir to prevent burning until it is thoroughly blended. Pour in the oyster juice gradually, add the milk, and when the mixture boils put in the oysters. Let them cook about two minutes until they are plump and the edges curl.

CLAM BROTH. Wash half a dozen hard shelled clams and place them in a kettle over the fire with six tablespoonfuls of boiling water. When the shells open remove them. Strain off the juice, season with salt and pepper and serve.

If liked, half a pint of milk can be added, with a little **butter** and flour to thicken it.

MUTTON BROTH. Cut two pounds of lean mutton into squares, removing every particle of fat. Cover with one quart of cold water, let it come to the boil, and simmer slowly two hours. Twenty minutes before it is taken up, add one tablespoonful of well washed rice. Put in salt and pepper to taste.

CHICKEN BROTH. Weigh the fowl, an old one is best, and to each pound allow one pint of cold water. Break the bones and cut the meat small. Cover with the water and add one tablespoonful of rice. After it comes to the boil, let it simmer for two hours. Strain, season with salt and a little pepper, and serve hot. Only half the fowl need be used at once.

CHAPTER VIII.

SOLID FOOD.

MILK TOAST.

CUT a thin slice of bread, toast **it** evenly a delicate yellow brown, put it on a hot plate, cut it in four pieces, removing the crust, and pour over it half a pint of boiling milk previously thickened with one teaspoonful of flour rubbed smooth with a little cold milk and boiled in it. Salt to taste.

Cream to be whipped should stand on the ice until thoroughly chilled, and be at least twenty-four hours old. Put **WHIPPED CREAM.** it in a cold bowl and beat with an egg-beater until it is solid. Sugar and any of the Royal Flavoring **Extracts** desired may be added before it is beaten. If old enough and cold enough it will become a solid mass in ten minutes. Do **not** skim out the froth nor lift out the beater until it is done.

It may be eaten alone, or with bread, or toast, and is a delicious addition to any of the following dishes.

One tablespoonful of cornstarch, one teacupful of boiling water, **LEMON CORN-STARCH.** one egg, sugar to taste, one teaspoonful of butter, juice and grated rind of half a small lemon. Mix the cornstarch with a little cold water, add the boiling water and let it boil ten minutes. Put in tne sugar and pour the mixture on the yolk of the egg well beaten. Add the lemon juice and grated rind. Pour into a small pudding dish and bake ten minutes. Beat the white of the egg with two tablespoonfuls of **sugar** and spread it on the top. Return the dish to the oven for **a few** moments to color the Meringue a delicate brown. **Serve cold.**

Half a pint of water, half an ounce of gelatine, **whites of two** **LEMON SPONGE.** eggs, a quarter of a pound of sugar, juice of one large lemon. Soak the gelatine in enough warm water to cover it until it is perfectly soft. Heat the half pint or water and poor over it. Add the sugar and lemon juice, beat in the egg, it being first well beaten. Let the mixture get very hot out not quite boil. Pour into the dish in which it is to be served.

Half a small box of gelatine, half a pint of cold water, eight **SNOW JELLY.** tablespoonfuls of boiling water, half a cup of sugar, **the** whites of two eggs, juice and grated peel of one lemon. Dissolve the gelatine in the boiling water. When cool; add the other ingredients except the eggs. When the mixture stiffens, add the whites of egg beaten to a froth, and beat all together until light like new fallen snow.

Make a custard with half pint of milk **and the yolks of the two** eggs, a little **sugar and** grated lemon peel, **and pour around the** snow jelly.

Dishes made with gelatine are better prepared the day before **RICE JELLY.** they are to be used. Boil a quarter of a pound of rice in one quart of water for an hour, strain off the water, sweeten to taste and add the juice of a small lemon. Pour into a mould to form.

COFFEE JELLY. One ounce of gelatine, three quarters of a pint of strong clear coffee, a quarter of a pint of cold water. Soak the gelatine in the water. Heat the coffee, sweeten to taste and pour it on the gelatine. Stir until perfectly dissolved and pour it into a mould. Serve surrounded with whipped cream.

LEMON JELLY. One ounce of gelatine, half a pint of cold water, half a cupful of sugar, the juice of one large lemon and enough cold water add d to it to make half a pint of liquid. Soak the gelatine in the water and dissolve it by setting the bowl containing it on the top of a boiling tea kettle. When dissolved, add the other ingredients, the sugar first, stir well and pour into a mould. It need not be boiled or strained.

COFFEE CUSTARD. **Twelve** tablespoonfuls of milk and four of strong coffee, sweeten to taste and let it come to the boil. Pour the boiling mixture on the well-beaten yolk of an egg. If boiled custard is desired, return it to the saucepan, set it on **the fire and** stir until it thickens, but do not **let** it boil or the egg **will curdle.** If a baked custard is preferred, instead of pouring the mixture into the saucepan, put it into a kitchen cup, set the cup in a pan of boiling water, and **put it in** the oven for ten or fifteen minutes until it **is set**

PLAIN CUSTARD. This can be made in the same way, using the yolk of an egg to half a pint of milk, sugar to taste, **and** any of the " Royal Flavoring Extracts,' as desired.

RICE PUDDING. Wash one tablespoonful of rice. Boil a pint of milk and pour over the rice. Let it cook for half an hour, stirring three times at intervals of ten minutes. Then add a tablespoonful of sugar. As the milk boils away, **fill up the** dish to the original quantity with hot milk. Cook two **hours in** all. This gives the rice a delicious flavor. Keep the dish **where it** will not burn while cooking.

RENNET CURD. Sweeten one pint of milk to taste, add four tablespoonfuls of Sherry, or a little of any of the " Royal Flavoring Extracts," or no flavoring at all if the taste of the milk is liked. Warm until the chill is taken off, **about the** same temperature as the milk is when it comes from the **cow.** Crush two "Rennecine Tablets" and dissolve in a tablespoonful of water and add to the milk, a little more if Sherry is used.

Stir thoroughly and set it away for the curd to form. Serve with plain or whipped cream.

ICE CREAM. **Sweeten a** pint of cream to taste and add vanilla, orange, lemon or rose "Royal Flavoring Extract." If this is too rich for the patient use half milk and add the whites of two eggs **beaten** with the sugar.

If a small ice cream freezer is not at hand one **can be readily** improvised by using any tin vessel with a tight fitting cover. Put the cream in this and have a larger jar or **vessel that will** hold it. Pack around it in the outside jar, ice and **salt in the** proportion of one-third of the latter to two-thirds of the former. While the ice cream is freezing, lift the cover from the inner vessel several times and scrape the frozen **cream** from **the** sides, beating the mixture thoroughly. **This** makes it smooth **and** velvety.

SHERBET. Half a tablespoonful of gelatine soaked in four tablespoonfuls of cold water, add four tablespoonfuls of boiling water, when dissolved, add half a cup of sugar melted in half a cup of cold water. Stir in a teacupful of orange juice and freeze like ice cream.

Lemon juice may be used instead, adding more sugar ; or the juice of raspberries, or strawberries. The syrup from canned peaches is delicious.

CHAPTER IX.

NURSING IN SPECIAL DISEASES.

THERE are some simple ailments that can be **successfully** treated by an inexperienced person without **the help of a** doctor ; but when there is any doubt whether **a case is** serious or not, he should always be sent **for.** It is a thousand times better to send for him ten times unnecessarily, than once to put it off until it is too late, and it saves money, time and strength in the end to have his advice early in the illness.

If rest, warmth and abstaining from solid food for ten or twelve hours, with a free movement of the bowels, does not bring about a change for the better, it is a case for the doctor, and he should be called at once.

INDIGESTION. *Symptoms :*--An almost constant, fixed pain, aching, heaviness, a sense of weight, fullness, or pressure and discomfort after eating.

Remedies :--Plenty of exercise, in the open air if

possible, using the arms and chest muscles as in sawing wood or
sweeping.

Soda Mint Tablets, two at intervals of ten minutes after eating
Peptonic Pills often afford relief when everything else fails. Take
one or two immediately after eating.

Fellows' Compound Syrup of Hypophosphites is of great use in
giving tone to the system.

"D. & L." Emulsion of Cod Liver Oil with Hypophosphites of Lime and Soda is also of great value in such cases.

The bowels should be regulated by a daily enema of hot water, or by some simple laxative as Campbell's Cathartic Compound.

Diet:—What agrees with one will not with another, so different kinds of food must be tried—such as Koumiss, **Peptonized** Milk, Oatmeal gruel or porridge, Cracked Wheat, Rye **Bread, soft boiled** or poached eggs, rare meat, raw beef scraped, **mixed with bread** crumbs, made into pats and heated through on **a gridiron ; baked** potatoes, broiled fish, rice pudding, or any simple **blanc mange.** Stimulants should be avoided, and tea or coffee used in **moderation.**

A good Malt Extract owing to the process it **has gone through, if** it has been carefully prepared is **a** capital **thing as it is at once** taken up by the system without taxing the digestive organs in the least. It is an excellent assistant **to** digestion **and a** "Nutritive Tonic." Wyeths is the best.

CON- STIPATION

This proceeds from a variety **of** causes, and various remedies must be tried.

Moist applications over the bowels may be tried.

A piece of flannel wrung out of warm water and squeezed as dry as possible, can be bound on with a broad bandage, and worn for two or three hours a day.

Kneading the Bowels :—Every morning before rising, the bowels should be pressed or kneaded, beginning low down on the **right** side working up across the abdomen and down the left **side, finishing** with a general pressing and rubbing of the whole **surface. The** operation should continue about ten minutes.

Fluid :—Sometimes a glass of cold water **before breakfast, and** another at ten o'clock will be effectual.

Diet :—Brown bread, Indian meal porridge **with** molasses, oatmeal, fresh fruit, vegetables, very little meat, stewed prunes and apples, figs soaked **over night and eaten** in the morning, and coffee **without** sugar.

DIARRHŒA

This is a symptom that the digestive tract is out of order, rather than a disease in itself. When it becomes chronic, it requires medical treatment, but if taken in time is seldom severe.

Remedies :—Rest in bed. A broad flannel bandage wound around the bowels. Abstinence from solid food, and a spoonful of Perry Davis' Pain-Killer in hot milk and water occasionally.

Diet:—Boiled milk and lime water, Rice water, Wheat flour gruel, Koumiss. Later, milk toast.

Medicine:—A dose **of** castor oil, from a dessertspoonful to a *tablespoonful*, to carry off the undigested food that is causing the trouble. If the movements are frequent, causing much distress, an enema of four *tablespoonfuls* of thin starch, with thirty drops of laudanum after each one.

**DYSEN-
TERY.**
This is an inflammation of the large intestine and more serious than diarrhœa.

Symptoms —A painful desire to have a movement without the power of accomplishing it. Blood in the motions. Great pain in the bowels.

Treatment:—Perfect rest in bed. Warm Pain-Killer applications to abdomen to relieve pain.

Medicine:—Compressed Ipecac and Opium Pills, five grains, once in four hours, will give relief.

Diet:—Boiled milk, rice water and rice gruel, all given luke-**warm.** Return very gradually to solid food.

**CHOLERA
MORBUS.**
Symptoms:—Violent pain in the intestines, cramps, vomiting and **diarrhœa.** The motions are a greenish yellow.

Treatment:— Vomit the patient with mustard and warm water if the trouble is due to indigestible food. Give at once a teaspoonful of Pain-Killer in a wine glass of hot water with a little sugar. Repeat the same dose every half-hour until the pain is relieved. Rub the stomach and bowels with the hand wet in Pain-Killer. Wring out flannels in very hot water to which a tablespoonful of Pain-Killer has been added, and put across the stomach and the bowels. Change them every twenty minutes. If there is much vomiting, settle the irritated stomach by drinking freely of hot water to a cupful of which a few drops of Pain-Killer have been added.

Diet:—The same as in diarrhœa when the patient is able to eat.

**BILIOUS-
NESS.**
Symptoms:—Nausea after eating, flatulence, distension of bowels, cold feet, pain in the back of neck, disagreeable taste in the mouth, depression of spirits, yellow tinge in white of eyes.

Remedies:—Abstinence from food for eight hours. A dose of "D. & L." Liver Pills repeated two or three times. A tumbler of soda-water every three hours, or even of plain cold water.

Diet :—No meat, plenty of vegetables, fresh fruit, especially grapes ; bread, tapioca or rice pudding, gruels, mutton broth, lemonade, no coffee.

Coryza is the technical term for a cold in the head. At the first symptoms of a bad cold, take a warm bath, go to **COLDS.** bed between blankets with a rubber hot water bottle at the feet, drink a tumbler of hot lemonade, **and** take a Compressed Dover Powder, five grains. If **the head feels** hot and oppressed, soak the feet for twenty **minutes in twelve** quarts of very hot water, with three tablespoonfuls of **mustard** stirred in it. If the mouth is dry, let a Chlorate of Potash **Lozenge,** **five** grains, dissolve in it once in three hours. If **this treatment** does not break it up, take a dose of D. & L. Liver **Pills, next night.** When the chest is sore, rub it with olive oil **or camphorated oil,** warmed in a teacup, set in boiling water. Cover it **with two thick-** nesses of flannel or cotton wool. Wear this for several days, **remov-** ing a small piece at a time. If there is much pain, apply a mustard paste, or what is better still a Pain-Killer compress. When there is a cough, Pyny Pectoral may be used to relieve it.

Diet :—Porridge, bread and milk, eggs, blanc mange, plain puddings. Avoid meats and stimulants for a time.

When a throat is slightly inflamed it can be cured by wringing a piece of cotton out of cold water, binding it on the **SORE** **THROAT,** neck all night and covering it with a strip of flannel. Sometimes a mustard poultice left on until the skin is well reddened will relieve, or a Pain-Killer compress **ap-** plied on going to bed.

If the throat is relaxed a gargle of alum and water **will relieve** it. If it feels rough and rasped, a teaspoonful of chlorate of potash, two tablespoonfuls of honey or glycerine stirred into **a** tumbler of water and used as a gargle is good. If the throat **seems** full of mucous, a dessertspoonful of salt dissolved in a glass of water is beneficial. All these gargles must be used at least once in half an hour to be of any use.

Diet :—Milk, egg nog, beef juice, **cocoa, gruel,** rare juicy meat, or any nourishing food that can be taken.

Acute rheumatism, or rheumatic fever, is excruciating, involving great suffering to the patient. The sufferer should **RHEU-** **MATISM.** lie between blankets and wear a flannel nightdress. There is always excessive perspiration. The body must be often rubbed off with warm soft towels, passing the hand under the night-dress to do it. A warm sponge bath of strong salt and water twice a day, morning and night, is good. The vessels and everything used about him must be warmed before **they are** introduced into the bed.

Diet :—Milk in every form in which it can be prepared, **as gruel** made with it, blanc mange, puddings, custard, koumiss, **eggs and** vegetable soups.

Persons who suffer from chronic rheumatism should wear red flannel next the skin day and night, avoid exposure to the cold, stimulants and meat diet, living on milk, eggs, vegetables and farinaceous food. Cooked apples, prunes and oranges are good, and lemonade and lime-juice as a drink. Give Anti-Rheumatic Tablets of Lithium and Potassium, following Elixir of Salicylic acid, or Salycilate of Soda Tablets, say ten grains twice a day.

NEURALGIA. This is often caused by constipation, and the bowels should be regulated by a gentle laxative. Campbell's Cathartic Compound will be found excellent for the purpose. "Wyeth's" Beef, Iron and Wine will give tone to the system ; or what might prove better still, " D. & L." Emulsion of Cod Liver Oil with Hypophosphites of Lime and Soda. A Rubber hot water bottle applied to the seat of pain gives ease. The application of a Menthol Plaster will drive it away ; or a Pain-Killer compress bound on.

Diet : **Plenty of milk, eggs and nourishing food. That prescribed for constipation will be of use. Meat may be eaten in moderation, if not fried.**

WORMS. Thread worms—Symptoms in children : fretfulness, itching of the anus and nose, pain in the stomach, occasionally convulsions and unconsciousness. The tiny worms, like pieces of white thread, are sometimes seen in the motions.

Remedies : Two teaspoonfuls of Castor oil every other night for three nights. Soak a tablespoonful of the chips of Quassia wood in a pint of water for an hour, strain it and add a tablespoonful of fine salt. With a bulb syringe inject a quarter of a pint of this infusion into the rectum every day until the whole is used.

Sometimes the worms are large, round and a very light brown. The best remedy for this species is Santonin. Give two Santonin and Chocolate Lozenges at bed time for two nights. After the worms **have** been expelled, small doses of the " D. & L." Emulsion of Cod **Liver** Oil, with Hypophosphites of Lime and Soda, which is sold **by** all druggists, should be given to build up the system, or " **Wyeth** " Liquid Malt Extract.

Diet : While the worms are present this should consist largely of milk. Afterwards meat, eggs and other nourishing food should be given.

CROUP. Parents whose children are liable to croup should keep in the house powders of Turpeth Mineral, three grains each, as this is the best emetic to use. A very convenient and excellent remedy is " Pyny Pectoral" when used according to directions which accompany each bottle.

Symptoms : Physicians divide this disease into true and false croup, but the early stages of both are much alike to the non-professional eye. The child wakens between ten and twelve o'clock with a loud, barking cough, great difficulty in breathing, flushed face, quick pulse and hot skin.

Treatment : Put the child at once into a hot bath. Give the emetic until it has vomited freely. Let it breathe the steam from a pitcher of boiling water, and if possible put a small lump of lime in the pitcher before pouring in the water. If the case is progressing favorably the child falls asleep, the face is less flushed, the pulse slower and the breathing easier. If this improvement does not take place within an hour, send for the doctor.

Dress the child in flannel, and do not let it go out in the cold or damp air for some days.

Diet : Give plenty of milk and gruels, beef tea and eggs. Avoid meat, too much candy, or any unwholesome food. Regulate the bowels to secure a movement every day.

DIPHTHE-RIA. Diphtheria is really a disease of the blood which shows itself in the throat. This is covered with a grayish white membrane. Symptoms : Feverishness, difficulty in swallowing, stiffness of the neck and swelling of the glands of the throat outside.

Treatment : Send for the doctor. There is no time for trifling with home remedies. Follow his directions exactly. Isolate the patient. Gargle the throat with chlorate of potash tablets dissolved in water, until the doctor comes. If there is not a camel's hair brush at hand make a little swab for applying lotions to the throat by twisting a clean rag on a piece of stick. See that these applications are put in the throat when it is left to you, and that food and medicine are swallowed.

Provide old soft cloths to receive the discharge from nose and mouth and burn them as soon as used. Disinfect everything that leaves the sick-room.

If there are broken places anywhere in the skin keep them covered with carbolized vaseline, especially about the nose and mouth.

Diet: This must be the most nourishing possible and concentrated on account of the difficulty in swallowing. Beef juice, beef extract mixed with an equal proportion of cream, milk and white of egg. If brandy is ordered give it in milk. Do not allow the patient to get out of bed or sit up without the Doctor's permission, even in convalescence, as there is danger of paralysis of the heart.

SCARLET FEVER. Symptoms: Headache and feverishness for two days, then a bright red rash appears, first on the face and neck. It spreads evenly over the surface of the skin, and is not raised to the touch as the rash of measles is. Fever runs high and the throat is sore. The rash is sometimes visible before it appears outside. It is not infectious until the throat begins to be sore.

Treatment : Isolate the patient. Keep him in bed, and the room at a temperature of 65°. Give him a warm sponge bath, avoiding exposure. As the disease progresses and the skin begins to peel, keep the body well rubbed with vaseline. Ventilation is very important, but draughts must be avoided. "Wyeth's" Liquid M lt Extract is an invaluable nutritive tonic for convalescents and does not only nourish but strengthens the system increasing the appetite and acting on other foods as a digestive. Convalescence is slow and many complications may occur. Watch the water that is passed, and report to the doctor if it diminishes in quantity. About three pints should be passed by an adult in twenty four hours. Let no symptom escape unnoticed, and mention to the doctor even those that seem trifling.

Diet : This must be liquid until the fever subsides ; milk, plain and with white of an egg, meat broths, koumiss, lemonade, plenty of cold water, not iced, pieces of ice to **suck.**

Symptoms: A cold in the head. After four days a rash appears on the forehead and face, soon extending to the body. **MEASLES.** It is a darker red than in scarlet fever and feels raised under the skin. The eyes and chest are the points of attack.

Treatment : **If** the eyes are weak keep the room darkened. Supply fresh **air, but** guard against draughts and sudden chills. The temperature should be 65°. Cold may bring on bronchitis. Isolate the patient **on** the first symptom, as it may be conveyed before the rash comes out. Give a warm sponge bath daily. Keep the chest protected and the bowels regulated.

Diet : Gruels, broths and milk while the fever is high, then toast, blanc mange, porridge and light puddings, finally digestible meats and vegetables. Flaxseed tea helps to relieve the cough. Avoid exposure to cold even when convalescence is well established. Have all clean clothing well aired before putting it on.

Symptoms : Headache, loss of appetite, pains in legs, bleeding at nose, a slight cough, fever. About the end of the **TYPHOID** first week the abdomen swells and sometimes there **FEVER.** is diarrhœa. In this case the motions are a yellowish color, like pea soup.

Treatment : Much depends upon the nursing. The precautions against **bed sores** must be taken from the start, the patient kept clean **and dry as** directed in Chapter IV.

Diet : Peptonized milk, milk and lime water, milk and white of egg, koumiss, **bu**ttermilk, beef juice, beef extract, mutton and chicken broth. **Give no** solid food without doctor's permission.

Disinfect the discharges, as the disease is communicated by their means. Keep the temperature at 65°. Pure air is of vital importance. Do not let the patient be excited or worried by visitors. If there should be a hemorrhage from the bowels in the doctor's absence, give an enema of starch four tablespoonfuls, laudanum sixty drops. Then give one teaspoonful of brandy in four of milk by mouth every fifteen minutes for two hours.

When convalescing nothing will build them up as quickly as "Wyeth's" Malt Extract.

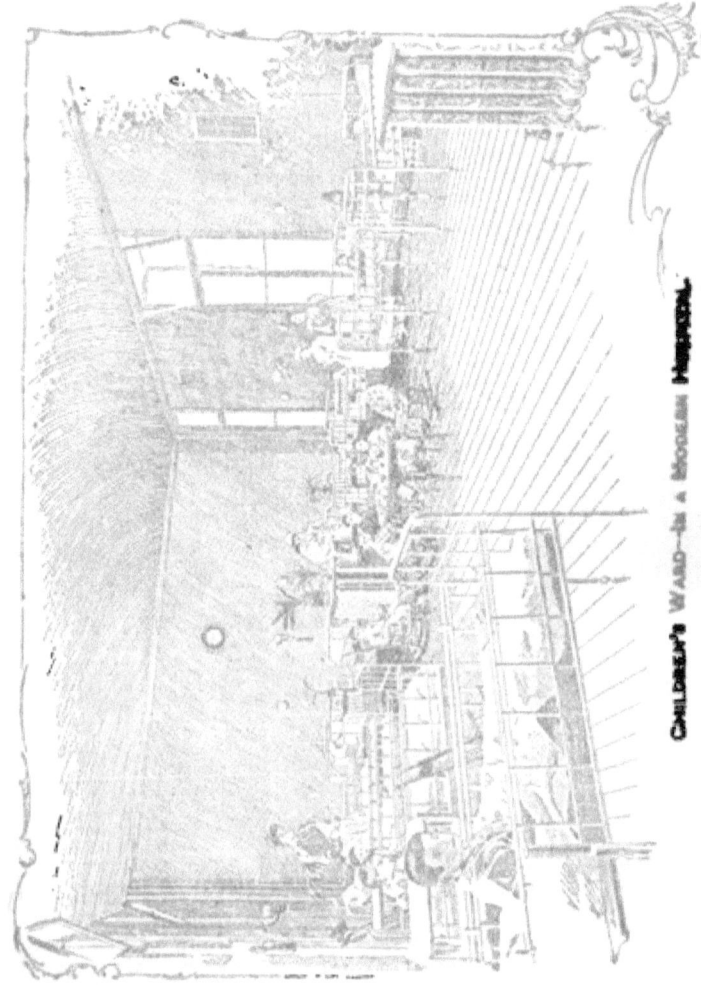

CHILDREN'S WARD—IN A MODERN HOSPITAL.

This is an inflammation of the lung itself.

PNEUMO-
NIA.
Symptoms: It begins with a chill, followed soon by fever. The breathing is oppressed, and sometimes there is pain in the chest and a cough. About the third day there is an expectoration of reddish mucous.

Treatment : Rub the chest with warm oil. Put on a poultice **jacket and cover the** chest with flaxseed poultices, never allowing **them to become cold.** The doctor will order medicine.

Diet : The same as in typhoid fever. When convalescing use Fellows' Compound Syrup of Hypophosphites it will aid in building up the system.

BRONCHI-TIS. This is **an** inflammation of the bronchial **tubes** through which the air is carried to the lungs.
Symptoms : The upper part of the chest is tight and sore. There is a hard dry cough.

Rub the chest well with warm oil, and cover it with two or three layers of cotton batting. Pyny Pectoral will be found useful and should be regularly taken. Give a do of Medicated Fruit Syrup if the bowels are constipated.

Diet · Milk in all its forms, beef juice and extract, **mutton and** chicken broths. Later, any light nourishing food.

Wyeth's Malt Extract to build up the system.

Fellows' Compound Syrup of Hypophosphites, is invaluable to patients recovering from Bronchitis. It nourishes the constitution and help the patient to regain strength and health.

PLEURISY. This is an inflammation of the **membrane** that lines **the chest** **and** covers the lungs.
Symptoms : Sharp pain in the side, great difficulty in breathing, cough and fever.

Treatment Apply **a** Pain-Killer compress or mustard plaster to relieve **the** pain Then rub the side with warm oil and cover it with flaun l. Give **a** Five Grain Compressed Dover Powder every half hour til three are taken. end for the doctor.

Diet : Same as in bronchitis

Fellows' Compound Syrup of Hypophosphites is of great **value** for giving tone to the system during convalescence.

CONSUMP-TION. Symptoms. Consumption in most cases comes on slowly with pains in chest, cough, perhaps bleeding from the lungs, debility and general wasting of the body
Occasionally it follows an acute attack of pneumonia **or** some other disease of the chest.

Treatment : Pure air and plenty of it, gentle exercise, nourishing food, tonics.

The value of Fellows' Compound Syrup of Hypophosphites in cases **of Consumption has been proven beyond question and its** peculiar **curativ character has been established with all who have** used it.

Pure air should be introduced into the sleeping room at night by having a fire if the air is cool, and then leaving the window open protected with a flannel as directed in Chapter II. Bad air is positive poison to consumptives. They should live out of doors **as** much as possible.

Diet : As much fat as can be digested in the shape of butter, cream, oil made into mayonaise or salad dressing, and the fat of meat. Peptonic Tablets will be found of great use in helping a delicate stomach to digest the fat, give three times a day. New milk warm from the cow, koumiss, raw eggs in every form, and milk should be freely used. The eggs can sometimes be taken beaten up with cold water. Poultry, fresh fish, beef and mutton are good. Pork and veal being indigestible should be avoided. Tomatoes, potatoes, young onions, and almost any fresh vegetables are beneficial. " Wyeth's " Liquid Malt Extract will be found a valuable agent to improve the appetite, fortifying the **system** and enabling it to better resist the effects of the desease.

SCROFULA. This is a disease which usually developes in childhood. It may be transmitted from the parents, or it may be caused by deprivation of pure air. The glands in neck, armpits or groins swell. There may be sores in different parts of the body, or the bones and joints may be affected.

Treatment : Sea air and salt water bathing, sunshine. Dr. Channing's Sarsaparilla is excellent for this, also the " D. & L." Emulsion of Cod Liver Oil and Hypophosphites of Lime and Soda, and " Wyeth's " Liquid Malt Extract. Wash with Palmo Carbolic Soap.

Diet : Cream, milk, butter, fresh meat, plenty of fat, eggs, fresh vegetables, oatmeal, brown bread.

MUMPS. Symptoms : Swelling of the glands below the ear. Taking an acid, as lemon juice or vinegar into the mouth causes acute pain in the gland, and is one method of determining whether the swelling is mumps or not. Any exposure to cold must be avoided. The swelling bathed in warm camphorated oil and wrapped in flannel. If there is much pain a flaxseed poultice can be applied. The bowels should **be** regulated with a gentle laxative, such as " D. & L." Liver Pill. **The** patient should be kept away from other children, as it is **infectious.**

Diet : Any light nourishing food that is easily **swallowed.**

WHOOPING COUGH. Symtoms : After about six days of langour and fretfulness the cough begins. It comes on in severe paroxysms, the child strangles and seems about to choke. It often vomits. The cough is infectious and lasts about six weeks.

Treatment : If there is no fever and the chest is not sore, the child should go out in fine weather. If the cough is tight and painful and not much mucous is spit out, give Compound Squill Lozenges. If the paroxysm is very violent, give Elixir Bromide of Ammonium, two teaspoonfuls. If the child is delicate, tonics will be required towards the close of the case. Wyeth's Liquid Malt Extract and the " D. & L." Emulsion of Cod Liver Oil with Hypophosphites are very good.

Diet : The most nourishing that can be taken, plenty of milk, **eggs,** oatmeal, and fresh meat.

CHAPTER X

ACCIDENTS AND EMERGENCIES.

TRY to fix a few general principles in the mind as to what to do when an accident happens, and then when the trial comes, keep cool and put them in practice.

In sending for the doctor, *write* a short statement of the case, that **he** may know what has happened, and **what** instruments and appliances to bring.

Keep always in the house an old sheet torn in strips about two inches wide, for bandages ; pieces of old linen, like the middle of pocket-handkerchiefs, or fine table linen, for wounds or burns ; a box of carbolic salve, a bottle of 'Perry Davis' Pain-Killer, a roll of Surgeons' rubber adhesive plaster, and a roll of absorbent cotton.

Wounds.—Wash the part well in cold water. If it is a clean cut, when the bleeding stops, draw the edges together **BLEEDING.** and strap with narrow strips of rubber plaster, leaving a space between each. Lay a piece of cotton wet in cold water over it, and fasten with a light bandage. After twenty-four hours dress it with carbolic salve spread on linen.

When the bleeding does not stop and the blood soaks through the bandage, it is probable that an artery is cut. Take off the dressings, raise the limb and bind a wet cloth tightly on the bleeding point. If the blood continues to drip, fold a hard ball or small round stone in a strip of cotton, place it on the inside of the limb, just under the swell of the muscle near the arm pit or groin, and tie the bandage tightly around the limb. A stick can be passed through the knot, and the bandage twisted to increase the compression. This brings the sides of the artery together, stops the blood and saves life. Carbolic salve, or Friar's Balsam, is the best **dressing** for **a** wound after the bleeding has stopped.

Raise the patient into a half sitting position with pillows. Give **BLEEDING** pieces of ice and apply an ice bag to the chest, or a **FROM THE** rubber hot water bag, filled with cold or ice water. **LUNGS.** Keep the sufferer properly quiet, allow no talking and show no alarm. The blood is bright red when coughed up.

This is an early symptom of typhoid fever, but often means **BLEEDING** nothing more than a little fulness in the head. Make **FROM THE** the patient lean back in a chair, and hold a wet **NOSE.** sponge to the nose to receive the blood. Wrap a piece of ice in flannel and hold it to the back of the neck. Sniff cold salt and water up the nostrils. If the flow is still alarming, send for the doctor, as the nose will have to be plugged.

If possible, raise the bruised part so that the blood will run away from it. Apply cloths wrung out of ice water, do **BRUISES.** not let them drip but change o ten to keep them cold. If there is much pain, bathe the affected part with Pain-Killer, and follow directions on each bottle.

Soak the part in water as hot as can be borne, adding more to keep up the heat for an hour. Then wrap it in flannel **SPRAINS.** wrung out of boiling water, lay a Rubber Hot Water bottle against it, and change as often as is necessary to keep it hot. After twenty-four hours wrap in dry flannel, still continuing the hot water bottle. "Perry Davis" Pain-Killer will help to relieve the pain. Apply it warm. The Compress is best. See page 11.

If air is **cut off** from fire **it cannot burn. Therefore** when a woman's clothes **take fire the first thought** should **BURNS.** be to smother it **as quickly as possible.** Any woollen material **wrapped around her will do this.** If none is at hand, roll her over **and over on the floor if there is no water** at hand. Tell her to keep **her mouth closed, so as not to swallow** the flame.

When the fire is out, drench the clothing **over the** burned parts and then *cut* it away. If patches stick, **do not** pull them off. Wring cloths out of baking soda stirred into water, cover the burns and keep them wet. Lay blankets on a bed with any water-proof covering over them, and lift the sufferer on them. If the body is much burned, raise the upper bed-clothes on boxes so as not to touch it. Cover the unburned parts with blankets. Give warm milk and brandy if the pulse is feeble from the shock. Send for the doctor as soon possible. Very nourishing food is needed.

A cloth wet in "Perry Davis" Pain-Killer and *kept wet* is a good remedy for a slight burn. After a few days it can be dressed with Vaseline.

Treat like burns. In most cases, covering the surface with "Perry Davis" Pain-Killer will give relief. Paint on several **SCALDS.** layers as each dries.
        If a child swallows boiling water give white of egg and milk, and pieces of ice to suck. Apply hot fomentations to throat until the doctor comes.

The heart ceases to act for one moment, **the supply of blood to** the brain is cut off, and the person **loses** conscious-**FAINTING.** ness. Lay him, or her, flat on the back. Lower the head, or raise the feet of the bed or sofa. Unfasten the clothing about the neck and waist. These measures are usually sufficient. If not, hold ammonia to the nose, press both hands on the chest and raise them quickly. Dash cold water in the face. Give a little strong stimulant. In desperate cases try artificial respiration.

In *Throat.*—Sometimes a smart slap on the back will dislodge it and send it down. It can be pushed down with the **FOREIGN** finger or a blunt stick ; if not too large. A fork and **BODIES.** the handle of a spoon, can be passed, one above and one below it to draw it out. Tickling the throat will cause vomiting, which will expel small substances.

In Nose.—A pinch of snuff, or a few grains of red pepper to excite sneezing will usually remove it. If not, bend the end of a piece of fine wire slightly, work it up behind the obstruction and hook it down.

In Ear.—Turn the head with the ear downwards, and give it a smart slap on the other side. If this does not succeed, syringe the ear gently with warm water from a bulb syringe and it will float out.

In the Eye.—Bathe the eye with warm water. Draw down the lower lid and if the particle that is causing the trouble can be seen, remove it, a fold of handkerchief over the head of a pin is a good instrument. If it is under the upper lid, lay a pencil outside the eye and turn the edge of the lid up over it, then take out the atom, If it is a speck of lime, or any alkali, bathe the eye in weak vinegar. If it is a drop of acid, wash it in baking soda and water. Keep down the inflammation by applying one thickness of cloth wrung out of ice water and not allowed to get dry.

In the Stomach.—Children often swallow tacks, marbles and other indigestible articles. Give a good meal of oatmeal porridge bread and milk, bread pudding, or any soft food and it will in all probability pass away without any trouble. Keep watch of the motions for a day or two, to see that it is discharged.

POISON-ING. When poison has been swallowed, the treatment must be prompt to be of any use. There are two classes of remedies to be administered, and whichever is most readily to be got should be given first, these are :—

1. Emetics.
2. Antidotes.

Get the poison out of the stomach as soon as possible by an emetic. Tickling the back of the throat with the finger, or a feather, will cause vomiting.

One tumbler after another of luke-warm water will do the same.

The principal classes of poisons are :—

Alkalies, as potash, ammonia, etc. For these, *acids* are the antidotes as vinegar, lemon juice, etc.

Acids as oxalic acid, carbolic acid, etc., for which *Alkalies* are the antidotes, as baking soda, lime water, magnesia, etc.

Acrid poisons ; as croton oil, alcohol, turpentine, etc., for which mucilages are the antidotes ; as gum arabic dissolved in warm water, starch dissolved in cold water and thickened with boiling water, arrowroot made in the same way, etc.

Irritant poisons ; as corrosive sublimate, arsenic, saltpetre, calomel, copperas, etc. The symtoms are much the same as in acrid poisons, but they affect the bowels more permanently. The antidote is albumen, as white of egg stirred into water, wheat flour in water, milk, etc.

Narcotic poisons, as opium in its various forms, such as lauda-num, paregoric, morphine, etc., tobacco, belladonna, digitalis, etc.

Give *strong* coffee, apply cold to head and warmth to feet, rub the limbs and supply fresh air. Try to keep the patient roused and awake.

General directions; It is always safe to give plenty of milk. If the poison was of an irritating nature, it soothes the inflamed membrane.

When the pulse is weak, give some stimulant, whiskey or brandy, mixed with water. If the mouth and throat are burned by the poison, give the stimulant as an enema mixed with an equal quantity of luke-warm milk. Use a bulb syringe and inject very slowly. Keep the patient in bed and perfectly quiet. When out of danger, give a dose of castor oil to carry off any traces of poison that may linger in the stomach or bowels.

Give light diet for a few days.

Do not keep liniments, which often contain poison, in the same place as medicines that are to be taken internally.

CHAPTER XI

DISINFECTION.

DISINFECTION can be thoroughly carried out with a very few disinfectants.

Boiling water, Corrosive sublimate, Sulphur, Copperas. It should be understood that pure air is the best disinfectant. If a case of infectious disease could be nursed out of doors there would be little need of disinfectants.

Supply warm air and keep the windows open as much as possible.

If the sick room communicates with another room, do not use the door from the sick room into the hall, but keep it locked, and pass through the adjoining room, where the windows should be always open. If there is only one door out of the sick room, hang a sheet over the doorway and keep it constantly wet with a solution of corrosive sublimate. Use as far as possible old clothing that can be burned. Have a tub half full of a solution of corrosive sublimate and into this put every article of clothing from patient, or bed, that is to be washed. After soaking in this for some hours, wring them out, and send them to the laundry, where they must be washed alone and *boiled*.

After a vessel has been used, before emptying it, fill it with copperas water, after emptying, wash it in hot water, rinse in cop-peras water, scald with boiling water, and leave it outside the sick room until it is needed again. Do not let cups, spoons, plates, or any dishes used in the sick room leave your hands until they are washed and rinsed in scalding water.

When the patient recovers, he must have a full bath of water, in which a pound of powdered borax has been dissolved and Palme

Carbolic Soap used his hair washed, and every article of clothing changed before he is allowed to mix with the family.

When the patient leaves the sick room, open the window and carry away soiled clothing to be disinfected. Put mattresses and pillows out in the sun, sprinkle them with corrosive sublimate solution, and after twenty-four hours send them to be made over.

Open drawers and closets. Take an old coal-scuttle, or good tin pan, without holes in the bottom, throw in some paper and shake over that two pounds of sulphur. Close windows and doors, and if they do not fit tightly, paste paper over the cracks, leaving one door open to go out by. Light the paper under the sulphur and leave the room. Paste the keyhole of this door, and if necessary the cracks, from the outside. In twenty-four hours go in and open the windows. When it is possible to breathe in the room, have the floor and woodwork washed, first with corrosive sublimate solution, then with plenty of hot water and soap. Have the walls scraped, washed with corrosive sublimate and re-painted or papered. The ceiling treated in the same way. Wash all the furniture and have any that is upholstered re-made.

In scarlet fever and small-pox it is safest to burn everything that cannot be boiled or treated as described.

After death from an infectious disease, the body should be washed in corrosive sublimate solution, a large napkin containing a pad soaked in it should be pinned around the hips, the body wrapped in a sheet wrung out of a solution of corrosive sublimate, and buried as soon as possible. No one should be permitted to see the remains.

> R. Corrosive sublimate solution.
> Fifteen grains of corrosive sublimate.
> Fifteen grains of muriate of ammonia.
> One quart of water.
> This makes a strength of 1 part to 1,000.

Wilson's Antiseptic Tablets, are a very convenient from, as they are already prepared for dissolving. One can be added to each pint of water.

> R. Copperas Water.
> Copperas four pounds.
> Hot water ten quarts.
> Stir with a stick until dissolved.

Throw handfuls of dry copperas down the water closet morning and evening, and flush it well afterwards.

If a dry closet is used, throw in shovelfuls of copperas and cover the surface with lime, dry earth or coal ashes.

The nurse should hold herself responsible for the prevention of the spread of infection, as, if she does her duty, it is impossible for it to extend beyond the case in hand.

N.B.—Caution must be taken as to the *extremely* poisonous character of these disinfectants.

PAIN-KILLER.

KNOWN THE WORLD OVER AS THE MOST USEFUL MEDICINAL PREPARATION IN EXISTENCE. SHOULD BE IN EVERY HOUSE.

JUST THE THING NEEDED AT HOME FOR ALL THE COMMON PAINS WE ARE SUBJECT TO. WORTH ITS WEIGHT IN GOLD IN CASES OF ACCIDENT OR SUDDEN ILLNESS.

PERRY DAVIS.

PAIN-KILLER A sure cure for Sore Throat, Coughs, Chills, Diarrhœa, Dysentery, Cramps, Cholera, and all Bowel Complaints.

PAIN-KILLER The best remedy known for Sea Sickness, Sick Headache, Pains in Back or Side, Rheumatism and Neuralgia.

PAIN-KILLER Is the Best Liniment made. It brings speedy and Permanent relief in cases of Bruises, Cuts, Sprains, Severe Burns, &c.

A PROMINENT MONTREAL CLERGYMAN'S ENDORSATION.

''Permit me to send you a few lines to strongly re-commend and endorse Perry Davis' Pain-Killer. I have used it with much satisfaction for the past thirty-five years and have also seen its good results in al-leviating pain in the different parishes in which I have lived. It is a preparation which deserves full public confidence.'' JAMES H. DIXON, Rector St. Judes and Hon. Canon of Christ Church Cathedral.

Montreal, December 22nd, 1896.

BEWARE !! When you ask for **PAIN-KILLER** some dealers will try and substitute something else. Do not take it. None Genuine save PERRY DAVIS'.

WYETH'S
BEEF, IRON & WINE.

THIS PREPARATION has been before the public now for more than a quarter of a century and has been freely prescribed by the physicians of Canada with most satisfactory results. The sales have been very extensive amounting to many millions of bottles.

ITS STIMULANT PROPERTIES.—In this preparation are combined the stimulant properties of Wine and the nutriment of Beef, with the tonic powers of Iron, the effect of which on the blood is so justly valued. For many cases in which there is Pallor, Weakness, Palpitation of the Heart, with much nervous disturbance, this article will be found especially adapted.

TO SUFFERERS FROM WEAKNESS.—It is a Nutritive Tonic, indicated in the treatment of impaired Appetite, Impoverishment of the Blood, and in all the various forms of General Debility. Prompt results will follow its use in cases of Sudden Exhaustion, arising either from acute or chronic diseases.

GROWING CHILDREN.—Especially those who are sickly, get great benefit from this preparation.

PEOPLE WHO ARE GETTING OLD, who find their strength is not what it used to be, experience a decidedly tonic effect from its use as occasion requires.

CLERGYMEN, TEACHERS and members of other professions, who suffer from weakness, you will find WYETH'S BEEF, IRON AND WINE very effectual in restoring strength and tone to the system after the exhaustion produced by over mental exercise.

OVERWORK.—Many men and women know that the continuous fatigued feeling they labor under is due to overwork, still they find it impossible just yet to take complete rest. To all such we would say use WYETH'S BEEF, IRON AND WINE.

NOTE—Physicians and patients have been much disappointed in the benefit anticipated, and often ill effects have been experienced from the use of the many imitations claiming to be the same, or as good as WYETH'S. In purchasing or prescribing please ask for "WYETH'S" and do not be persuaded to take any other.

Fellow's Compound Syrup

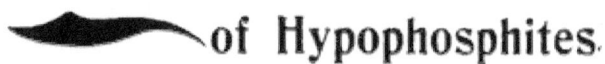of Hypophosphites.

NOTICE-CAUTION.

THE success of FELLOWS SYRUP OF HYPOPHOSPHITES has tempted certain persons to offer imitations of it for sale. Some of these falsely assert to having been in our employ, where the mode of preparing the genuine Syrup was obtained. Mr. Fellows, who has examined samples of several of these mixtures, **finds that no two of them are identical,** and that all of them differ from the original in composition, in freedom from acid reaction, in suscep tibility to the effects of oxygen when exposed to light and heat, **in the property of retaining the strychnine in solution,** and in the medicinal effects.

As a precaution, it is advisable that the Syrup should be purchased in the original bottles; the distinguishing marks which the bottles (and the wrappers surrounding them) bear, can then be examined, and the genuineness—or otherwise—of the contents thereby proved.

For sale by all Druggists in the Dominion.

DAVIS & LAWRENCE CO., Ltd.,

SOLE AGENTS FOR THE DOMINION OF CANADA.

MONTREAL.

PERRY DAVIS' PAIN=KILLER.

Opinions of Prominent People.

There is an old saying that "the proof of the pudding is in the eating" the same simile might be truthfully applied to medicines, the efficacy of which are only tested by those who have tried them and have been benefitted by them. Perry Davis' Pain Killer has been in use now for nearly sixty years by all peoples and in every part of the globe. The flattering words which have been said for this remedy are not exaggerated and their genuineness are guaranteed by the thousands of letters we have received lauding its praises. We subjoin the following which are a few of the numerous ones received.

The Story of Capt. J. F. Clarke, Police Force, Montreal.

"I have used Perry Davis' Pain Killer on several occasions and have found it very valuable in cases of sudden pains in the stomach. I accompanied the Royal Engineers on the Red River Expedition about 30 years ago under Col. Wolseley and on that occasion did not omit to take a supply of this grand medicine and was thankful for it before many days had passed. Owing to drinking bad water the men were often seized with cramps and by using Pain Killer the pain was always removed and it was found to be the most precious article in camp and worth its weight in gold. We use it here in No. 7 Station and I can with confidence recommend it to any one suffering from pain."

March 1st, 1897.

JAS. F. CLARKE,
Capt. No. 7, Police Division.

A well known Clergyman's Views.

"I have known your Pain-Killer for many years and have much pleasure in testifying to its valuable properties in alleviating pain. I consider it a most useful preparation."

December 16th, 1896.

(Rev.) H. J. EVANS,
497 St. Urbain St., Montreal.

Nothing like it in the World.

"I have been using your Pain-Killer for the last four years and I am satisfied that there is nothing like it in the world for cramps and all stomach troubles."

January 12th, 1897.

(Mrs) JAMES McMURRAY,
Black Brook, N.B.

A Preparation of great Virtue.

"I may say that from my own personal knowledge of Pain-Killer I have found it without doubt one of great virtue giving general satisfaction both as to its sale and use. For neuralgic pains, cramps, colic, and all bowel complaints, toothache, etc., it is far ahead of all others. Farmers and everybody living at a distance from a doctor or druggist should keep a bottle of Perry Davis' Pain-Killer in the house at all times. It will save many a doctor's visit."

October 14th, 1896.

EDMUND JENNER, Sherbrooke Drug Store.
Sherbrooke, N.S.

A Wonderful cure Effected.

"Last winter my wife was suffering intense pain from the effects of a paralytic stroke in her side and but for the application of your Pain-Killer at the most critical stage of her illness she would have lost her life. This was endorsed by the doctor attending her at the time. I cannot say too much for Pain-Killer and would not be without it in the house."

October 24th, 1896.

JOB LUCIER,
McGregor, Ont.

Do not delay getting a bottle of this valuable medicine but secure one at once an'l have it handy for cases of emergency or sudden attacks of pain. See that you get the genuine and avoid all substitutes which are frauds. Ask for

PERRY DAVIS' PAIN=KILLER.

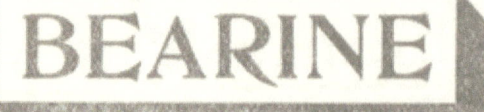

AN EPICURE'S DELIGHT is to have his Deserts Flavored with

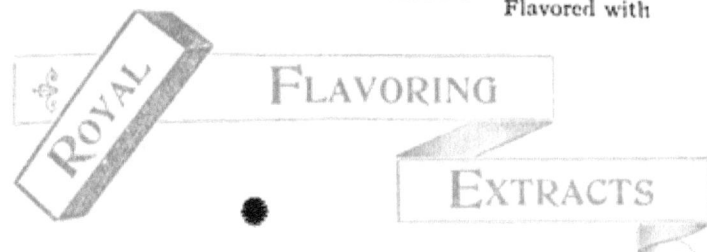

ROYAL FLAVORING EXTRACTS

They are superior to any made and there superiority consists in their PERFECT PURITY and GREAT STRENGTH. They are also more economical than ordinary flavoring extracts as a lesser quantity will be sufficient.

ICE CREAM, RUSSES and CUSTARDS are made perfect by its use.

SOME OF THE FLAVORS:

LEMON, ORANGE, ROSE, CLOVER, VANILLA, PEPPERMINT, CINNAMON, ALMOND AND WINTERGREEN.

Consumers will find it to their advantage to buy the larger sized bottles as shown herewith :—

SMALL SIZE,	or 25c. bottle,	contains 1¾	ounces	Liquid
QUARTER PINT SIZE,	or 50c.	"	"	4	"	"
HALF PINT SIZE,	or 75c.	"	"	8	"	"

If you cannot secure them from your dealer write direct to us.

DAVIS AND LAWRENCE CO., Limited, Montreal and New York.

A MOST VALUABLE REMEDY for the diseases of HORSES, CATTLE, SHEEP and POULTRY is

Condition "Maud S." Powders.

Many VALUABLE ANIMALS have been saved by their use.

A WELL KNOWN STOCK BREEDERS EXPERIENCE.

GENTLEMEN.—Please send me at once one hundred packages more of your "Maud S." Condition Powders. I do not want to run out, as I would not be without them on any account. I have used them for a long time, and have great faith in their efficacy for the various diseases for which they are recommended. Besides using for my cattle and horses, I employ them with great benefit in my poultry yard. As you are aware, I raise a large number of hens and other fowl, and I have proved to my entire satisfaction that there is nothing to equal the "Maud S." Condition Powders for keeping them in a perfectly healthy condition.

JOHN IRVINE, Milkman and Stock-Breeder, Westmount, Montreal.

One package of "Maud S." Condition Powders contains more real medicinal virtue than twice its weight of any other Powder.

Reduced prices, ½ lb. Tins, 25 cts. ¼ lb. Packages, 15 cts.

SOLD EVERYWHERE.

DAVIS & LAWRENCE Co., Limited, Montreal and New York.

N. B.—If your dealers does not keep these write direct to us.

AN EFFECTUAL
HEALTH RESTORER AND BLOOD PURIFIER
DOCTOR
CHANNING'S SARSAPARILLA.

Will CURE the worst form of SKIN DISEASE, Rheumatism, Salt Rheum, Pimples and Blotches, Scurvy, Dyspepsia, Boils and Humors. Will restore the Appetite and Renew the System. Is successful when other remedies fail and is recommended by Leading Physicians.

SOLD BY ALL MEDICINE DEALERS.

Price $1.00 per bottle.   **Six bottles $5.00.**

N B.—See that you get "DR CHANNING'S" and that other substitutes not as good are not forced upon you.

ALWAYS THE SAME A STANDARD OF WORTH ! ! !

An Indispensable TOILET ARTICLE for the LADIES.

HIND'S

HONEY AND ALMOND

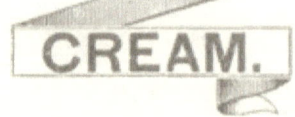

CREAM.

Soothing and Refreshing For Gentlemen After Shaving.

UNEXCELLED FOR SUNBURN AND CHAPPED SKIN

"I have used your HONEY & ALMOND CREAM for a long time in families where I have been called, and consider it invaluable for chafing and irritation of infants. I invariably recommend it in preference to anything else, and have always derived great satisfaction from its use.
MRS. H. J. POTTER, *Nurse*,
124 Emery St., Portland, Me.

"Three weeks ago I came home from the beach with my face and arms covered with sores caused by the sun and salt water while in bathing. A week ago I began to use your wonderful HONEY & ALMOND CREAM, and to-day my face is as smooth and soft as one could wish. I think your Cream is *simply wonderful.*"
ELLA L. FRIEND, Nashua, N. H.

A LEADING OPERA SINGER,—I consider your HONEY & ALMOND CREAM the best Cream I have ever used for the complexion.
CAMILLE D'ARVILLE.

PRICE 50 CENTS. FOR SALE BY ALL DRUGGISTS.

DAVIS & LAWRENCE Co., Limited. Montreal and New York

Convulsions. stiffening before
spasms. — due to con-
gestion of brain
cold especially at the back
of the neck or head.
Seat of vital processes at that
place. Empty bowel.
administer injection.
Soap & water or glycerine.
Removed to keep body warm
and head cool.

äet.
äl.

milk eggs, eggnogs custards
cream soups, sweet breads
fish meats cheese peas beans
lentils
B, Chiefly energy producing foo
1 Those rich in starch or sugar
Potatoes rice, macaroni, starchy
desserts, bread cake all sweets
peas beans, cereals
2 Those rich in fat or oil
Cream butter olive oil
mayonnaise, cooked salad dres
cheese ice cream walnuts egg yol
C Foods which keep the body in
good working order
a Fruits vegetable
b Coarse cereals preparation
ie bran muffins, graham brea
brown meal porridge
D. Water

Real nursing
Temperature, pulse, respiration
disturbances of blood
— make patient comfortable
and prepare for doctor
Administration of medicines
etc — care of surgical cases

Pe | 1906 |
Jan 2 | Communion Wine | . 1 6

Physical

Lungs, fresh air, free brea-
bowels regular —— not
skin

Kidneys plenty of good water
vegetable fruit & exercise
Plenty of fresh sleep

Bowels require work o

If possible 2 glasses of water between
meals. Acts on the skin with salt or
lemon to very cleansing.

Hygiene of home

Plenty of sunshine no flies

⅓ of day for sleep
Eat milk slowly eaten
cleanliness in all makes
for perfect health

Obstruction of fatty glands causes rough and
pimpled skin

CAIRNCROSS & LAWRENCE,
Prescription Chemists,

ELEPHONE 258. 216 DUNDAS ST., COR. PARK AVE.,
BRANCH: Branch LONDON, ONT.
DR. RICHMOND & PICCADILLY STS.
TELEPHONE 415.

SUNDAY HOURS { 10 to 11 a.m.
{ 2 to 4 p.m.
{ 8 to 9.30 p.m.

il Line,

For Rev Mr Watkins

℞ Bismuth Subnit ʒi

Lactopepsin ʒii

Acidi Lactici ʒss

To Nuso Vom ʒii

Spts Chloroform ʒvi

To Camphlo ʒiv

Aquam ad ʒiv

Sig. ʒi in ʒiv water 3 or
4 times a day a.c.

℞ W H Moorhouse

Paid
06
2

P,
Li.
Bi
St
1/2
2
F.
B

If possi
meals
lemon,
7

cleanliness in all makes
for perfect health

Obstruction of fatty glands causes rough and
wrinkled skin

"Allan" Royal Mail Line.

R.M.S.

Addresses. F. T. Lawrence
C/o Messrs Holt & Co
3 Whitehall Place, S.W.
Shaw' monument in Boston
Common & Curtis Boston.

Sam? Cowie / See Board of Trade
Edmonton, Peace River District.
Edward Berwick Pacific Grove, Cal.
W. H. Brown Moosomin, Assa.
N.W.T.

Garlic.. dry bulb - cut up
fine: make poultice in ...
large as palm of hand, off &
...

pat of skin —
old ... don't I
right occuring

24 James

ry of Meleg the
els Melville So
senna there